Ladybird Readers

Topsy and Tim
Go to London

Series Editor: Sorrel Pitts
Text adapted by Sorrel Pitts
Illustrated by Belinda Worsley

LADYBIRD BOOKS

UK | USA | Canada | Ireland | Australia
India | New Zealand | South Africa

Ladybird Books is part of the Penguin Random House group of companies
whose addresses can be found at global.penguinrandomhouse.com.
www.penguin.co.uk   www.puffin.co.uk   www.ladybird.co.uk

Penguin
Random House
UK

First published 2017
001

Copyright © Jean and Gareth Adamson, 2017

The moral rights of the author and illustrator have been asserted.

Printed in China

A CIP catalogue record for this book is available from the British Library

ISBN: 978–0–241–29743–8

All correspondence to:
Ladybird Books
Penguin Random House Children's
80 Strand, London WC2R 0RL

Ladybird Readers

Topsy and Tim
Go to London

Based on the story
by Jean and Gareth Adamson

Topsy  Tim

twins

Mommy  Dad

boat

playground

Tower of
London

train

Big
Ben

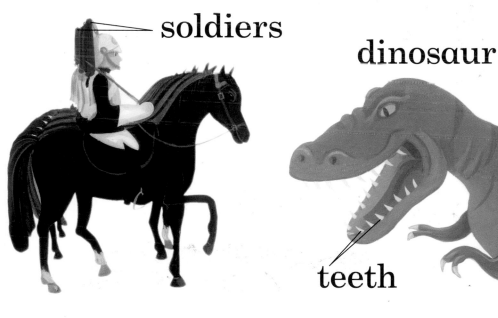

soldiers

dinosaur

teeth

5

Topsy and Tim are twins.
They have the same birthday.

They are going to London
with Mommy and Dad.

On Monday, Topsy and Tim see the Tower of London.

"It's very big!" says Topsy.

"We like the Tower
of London," says Tim.

On Tuesday, the twins
go on a train under
the streets.

Mommy wants to see
the horses and soldiers.

"The horses are
very big!" says Tim.

"The soldiers are
great!" says Topsy.

On Wednesday, Topsy and Tim go on a boat.

"I can see a big clock," says Topsy.

"That clock is Big Ben," says Mommy.

The boat goes to a big park.
Topsy and Tim enjoy
playing there.

On Thursday, Topsy and Tim see dinosaurs.

"This dinosaur is great!" says Topsy.

One dinosaur has got very big teeth!

Topsy and Tim do not like it!

"That dinosaur has got very big teeth!" says Tim.

On Friday, Topsy and Tim
go to a big playground.

They like playing
in the playground.

"I like this big
boat," says Tim.

Topsy and Tim go home.

"London is great!" says Tim.

"Our home is great, too!"
says Topsy.

Activities

The key below describes the skills practiced in each activity.

 Spelling and writing

 Reading

 Speaking

 Critical thinking

 Preparation for the Cambridge Young Learners Exams

1 Look and read. Put a ✓ or a ✗ in the boxes.

1  This is Topsy and Tim. ✓

2  This is Dad. ☐

3   This is Mommy. ☐

4  This is a dinosaur. ☐

5 This is a soldier. ☐

2 **Look at the letters.**
Write the words.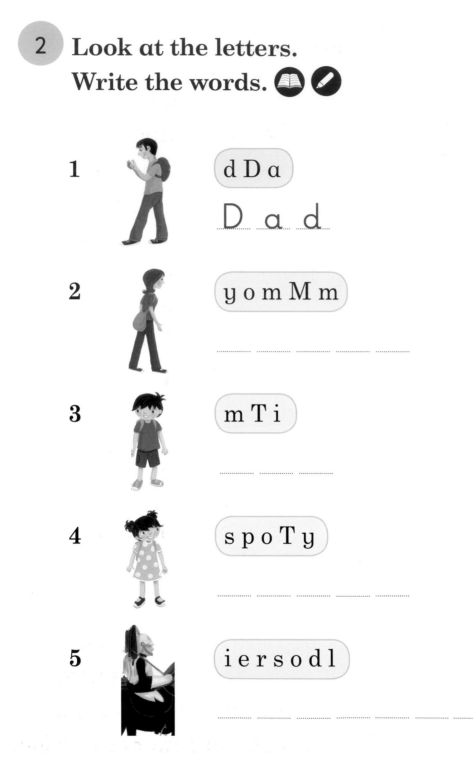

1   d D a

D a d

2   y o m M m

_____ _____ _____ _____

3   m T i

_____ _____ _____

4   s p o T y

_____ _____ _____ _____

5   i e r s o d l

_____ _____ _____ _____ _____

3 Circle the correct sentences.

1
   a Mommy and Dad are twins.
   b Topsy and Tim are twins.

2
   a Topsy and Tim are in London.
   b Topsy and Tim are at home.

3
   a Topsy and Tim see Big Ben.
   b Topsy and Tim see the Tower of London.

4
   a Topsy and Tim like the Tower of London.
   b Topsy and Tim do not like the Tower of London.

4 **Look and read. Write *yes* or *no*.**

1

This is the Tower
of London.   yes

2

This is a dinosaur.

3

This is a train.

4

This is Big Ben.

5

These are teeth.

5 **Ask and answer questions about the picture with a friend.** 🗨 ✦

Mommy wants to see the horses and soldiers.

"The horses are very big!" says Tim.

"The soldiers are great!" says Topsy.

1 How many children are there?

There are two children.

2 How many mommies are there?

3 What are the soldiers sitting on?

4 What can the twins see?

6 Find the words.

Tuesday
streets
train
twins
under

x y s T u e s d a y k h d t w i n s m b n t r a i n u r u n d e r w t s t r e e t s m

7 **Look and read. Circle the correct words.**

Mommy wants to see the horses and soldiers.

"The horses are very big!" says Tim.

"The soldiers are great!" says Topsy.

1 There are lots of soldiers and
horses. / **birds.**

2 Mommy wants to see the
soldiers. / **birds.**

3 "The horses are very big!"
says **Topsy.** / **Tim.**

4 The twins **like** / **do not like**
the horses.

5 "The **horses** / **soldiers**
are great!" says Topsy.

8 **Look and read. Choose the correct words and write them on the lines.**

On Wednesday, Topsy and Tim go on a boat.

"I can see a big clock," says Topsy.

"That clock is Big Ben," says Mommy.

boat   blue   clock   Big

1 On Wednesday, Topsy and Tim go on a ___boat___.

2 "I can see a big _____," says Topsy.

3 "That clock is _____ Ben," says Mommy.

4 The boat is _____.

9 **Match the two parts of the sentences.**

The boat goes to a big park. Topsy and Tim enjoy playing there.

On Thursday, Topsy and Tim go to see dinosaurs.

"This dinosaur is great!" says Topsy.

1 Topsy and Tim are in London

2 The boat goes to a

3 Topsy and Tim enjoy

4 Topsy and Tim

5 "This dinosaur is great!"

a playing there.

b see dinosaurs.

c says Topsy.

d big park.

e with Mommy and Dad.

10 Write the missing letters. 📖 ✏️

On Wednesday, Topsy and Tim go on a boat.

"I can see a big clock," says Topsy.

"That clock is Big Ben," says Mommy.

---

o a   e e   m m   a y

---

1 It is Wednesd a y.

2 On Wednesday, Topsy and Tim go on a b_____t.

3 "I can s_____ a big clock!" says Topsy.

4 "That clock is Big Ben," says Mo_____y.

38

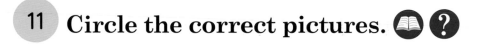

11 Circle the correct pictures. 📖 ❓

1 This can fly.

a   b

2 This goes under streets.

a   b

3 This goes on water.

a   b

4 These have got teeth.

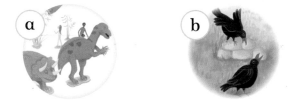

a   b

12 Who says this? 📖 ✏️ ✪

Topsy   Tim   Mommy

1 "We like the Tower of London,"

says _____Tim_____.

2 "The horses are very big!"

says _____.

3 "The soldiers are great!"

says _____.

4 "That clock is Big Ben,"

says _____.

5 "Our home is great, too!"

says _____.

13 Do the crossword. 📖 ✏️

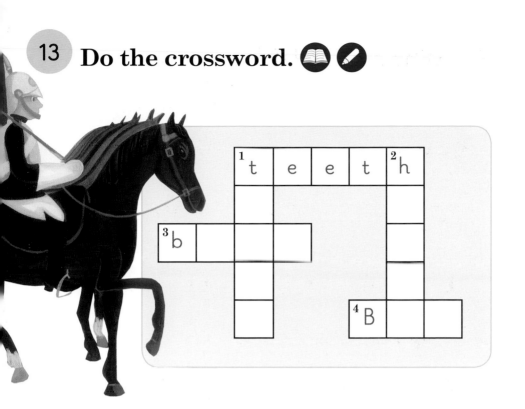

Across

1 Dinosaurs eat with these.

3 Tim plays on this in the playground.

4 The clock in London is Big . . .

Down

1 This goes under the streets of London.

2 A soldier sits on this.

14 **Write *go on*, or *go to*.** ✏️ 📖

1 Topsy and Tim ⎯⎯ go to ⎯⎯
London.

2 Topsy and Tim ⎯⎯⎯⎯⎯⎯⎯
a train under the streets.

3 Topsy and Tim ⎯⎯⎯⎯⎯⎯⎯
a boat.

4 Topsy and Tim ⎯⎯⎯⎯⎯⎯⎯
a park.

5 Topsy and Tim ⎯⎯⎯⎯⎯⎯⎯
a big playground.

15 **Order the story. Write 1—5.**

.... On Friday, Topsy and Tim go to a big playground.

___1___ On Monday, Topsy and Tim see the Tower of London.

.... On Thursday, Topsy and Tim see dinosaurs.

.... On Wednesday, Topsy and Tim go on a boat.

.... On Tuesday, the twins go on a train under the streets.

16 Work with a friend. You are Topsy. Your friend is Tim. Ask and answer questions about London. 💬 ❓

1

Do you like London?

Yes, I do.

2 Do you like the Tower of London? Why? / Why not?

3 Do you like the soldiers and the horses in London? Why? / Why not?

4 Do you like Big Ben? Why? / Why not?

17 **Read the questions. Write short answers.** 📖 ✏️ ❓

1 Who is Tim's twin?

Topsy

2 How many days are Topsy and Tim in London?

3 What do you think is Topsy and Tim's favorite day in London?

4 Do Topsy and Tim like their home?

18 Put a ✓ by the things Topsy and Tim see in London. 📖

Topsy and Tim go home.
"London is great!" says Tim.
"Our home is great, too!" says Topsy.

1 dinosaurs ✓

2 big teeth ☐

3 flowers ☐

4 a clock ☐

5 horses ☐

6 soldiers ☐

7 boats ☐

8 a train ☐

9 dogs ☐

10 a bus ☐

11 birds ☐

12 a cake ☐

13 people ☐

14 trees ☐

19 Draw a picture of your favorite place. Read the questions and write the answers. 📖 ✏️

1 What is your name?

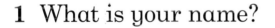

2 Where is your favorite place?

3 Why is it your favorite place?

Level 1

Anansi Helps a Friend	978-0-241-25409-7 ☐
Cinderella	978-0-241-25407-3 ☐
The Enormous Turnip	978-0-241-25408-0 ☐
On the Farm	978-0-241-25413-4 ☐
Cars	978-0-241-28354-7 ☐
Jon's Football Team	978-0-241-25411-0 ☐
The Magic Porridge Pot	978-0-241-25406-6 ☐
In the Garden	978-0-241-26220-7 ☐
Fun with Old Things	978-0-241-26219-1 ☐
Fairy Friends	978-0-241-28351-6 ☐
Peter Rabbit Goes to the Island	978-0-241-25415-8 ☐
Topsy and Tim Go to the Zoo	978-0-241-25414-1 ☐
Topsy and Tim Go to the Farm	978-0-241-28355-4 ☐
The Fair	978-0-241-28357-8 ☐
Daddy Pig's Old Chair	978-0-241-28356-1 ☐
Rex the Big Dinosaur	978-0-241-29741-4 ☐
Peter Rabbit and the Radish Robber	978-0-241-29742-1 ☐
Topsy and Tim Go to London	978-0-241-29743-8 ☐
On a Boat	978-0-241-29744-5 ☐
Baby Animals	978-0-241-29745-2 ☐

Now you're ready for Level 2!